STEVIE WONDERBOY

Kevin Scott

authorHOUSE®

AuthorHouse™ UK Ltd.
500 Avebury Boulevard
Central Milton Keynes, MK9 2BE
www.authorhouse.co.uk
Phone: 08001974150

First published by AuthorHouse 12/7/2009

ISBN: 978-1-4490-5839-5 (sc)

This book is printed on acid-free paper.

CHAPTER 1

The story begins with ex-professional footballer, Jimmy Howe. Jimmy Howe and his wife, Yvonne, were desperately trying for a child. They had tried for several years but to no avail. Jimmy used to be a top footballer for his local premiership club, Middleston FC, and was touted to become an England international in the making. However, Jimmy suffered a terrible injury in only his first season in the first team. The injury was so severe he was forced to retire from football at the young age of 21. He was totally devastated and found solace in drinking alcohol. His life was slowly going downhill. He had received a substantial amount of money from his PFA Pension, but soon his football pals started to dwindle away. Everyone seemed to of left him, apart from Yvonne who stood by him throughout everything.

Jimmy had a cousin who was in the building trade, his name was Gary. Gary could see that Jimmy was going through a bad time in his life, and wanting to help, he made an offer of a partnership in his building company business. The only catch was that Jimmy would have to invest some cash to purchase new vans, tools, etc. Jimmy knew nothing about the building trade but he trusted Gary completely so with most of his cash from his PFA Pension, he went into business with him. Due to there new vans and with plenty of advertising the

business was soon up and running well. They landed a huge contract with a big national house building
company and went from strength to strength. Things
were going so good that Jimmy had stopped drinking
and he and Yvonne got married and decided to try for
a baby.

After several years of trying, Yvonne was finding it
extremely hard to get pregnant. Until one day whilst
Jimmy was at work, Yvonne called him to give him
the good news she was with her doctor and he had
confirmed that she may be pregnant, Jimmy was ecstatic and he rushed home from work to celebrate,
and sure enough 3 weeks later after further test it was
confirmed she was pregnant. There prayers had been
answered! Jimmy and Gary's building company had
a won a contract with a major chemical company to
build a new depot that could set them up for life. Another celebration!

Jimmy counted down the days until his baby was born,
secretly he wanted a little boy who he hoped would
play soccer just like he used to, and on sat 28 July,
Yvonne gave birth to a little boy. He was 10 weeks
premature and only weighed 5 lbs 6oz. The nursing
staff had some concerns with him being so premature,
so he spent the first 3 weeks of his life in an incubator.
When he became strong enough to come home, Jimmy had made ready his new baby's bedroom, and of
course it had a football theme to it from the wallpaper
to the curtains. They decided to call the baby Steven,
after Yvonne's dad, and so there life was more or less
perfect. Jimmy was so proud of being a dad, he would
tell all his friends that one day his boy would play for
Middleston FC and England.

CHAPTER 2

A few years had gone by and Jimmy and Gary's business was going extremely well. They were nearing completion of the building of the new depot for the chemical company. As it seemed, life couldn't get any better. One lovely evening Jimmy said to little Steven, "come on son I want to take you to a special place". He picked little Steven up and placed him on his shoulders and set off to this special place. Just outside of town there was a wood the locals called "Ghostie wood", every one used to say it was haunted by strange white shapes but Jimmy loved it there. In fact Jimmy's own dad used to take him there when he was a youngster. In the centre of the wood was a clearing were there were no trees and nothing seemed to grow there, it was a round area about 100 meters in diameter and Jimmy loved it there. It was so quiet and tranquil and even little Steven seemed to love it there once they had arrived.

They stayed there for about an hour, until it started to get dark so jimmy picked up Steven and took him home. The following weekend was a special day it was little Stevens 5th birthday Jimmy had invited all of his family to his party, plus jimmy and Gary's building firm had been paid from the chemical company for all there hard work in building there new depot, so it was going to be a double celebration. The party went well but one thing Jimmy did notice was that Gary never showed up, so Jimmy rang Gary's phone but no one answered. Jimmy thought no more about it and the following day went to work as usual, but the yard was locked up with padlocks, Jimmy tried to ring Gary again but this time his phone relayed a message that said the number was no longer in use. Jimmy managed to break the padlocks off and then went to the office but to his surprise the office was bare. No computers, no desks, no chairs, no phones, it was stripped bare. Jimmy immediately thought they had been robbed so he rang the police, he then rang the office girls and several members of his work staff to see where they were and if they could shed any light on what had happened.

They all turned up for work as usual and were as much in the dark as Jimmy was. He knew Gary enjoyed his holidays in the sun in fact he had spoken about maybe one day moving abroad to live, suddenly Jimmy had a strange sensation in the pit of his tummy. He immediately rang the bank to check on the company's bank account, he froze in fear when the bank explained to him they needed to speak to him in person, he drove to the bank immediately. He was told he would have to speak to the branch manager, Mr Reynolds. He waited still not knowing what to expect, and 5 minutes later he was called in to Mr Reynolds office. Mr Reynolds informed Jimmy his company had no funds at all in the account, because the previous week Gary had closed the account and withdrew every last penny. He had obviously forged Jimmy's signature to do this and Jimmy was in total shock. He had left Gary in charge of the firm's finances because he trusted Gary implicitly. Jimmy went back to his yard , to find two burly men stood outside , they introduced themselves as bailiffs , they explained that they had come to take away the 2 company vans , for which the repairs and fuel bills had not been paid for several months, but the vans were no where to be seen, he later found out from friends that Gary had sold 2 vans to a local garage in the town. For the next few weeks Jimmy spent all of his time sorting out the financial mess Gary had left him in, he paid everyone that the company owed including his staff, he had to use up all of his savings just to break even. Jimmy was totally devastated all he had worked so hard for was gone; he sat down in his empty deserted yard and cried. The whole situation came to light several weeks later when he found out that Gary had put a deposit down on a villa in northern Cyprus months ago and had told his parents he may be leaving the UK, but told them not to tell anyone. Jimmy approached Gary's parents and they told him everything. Jimmy started to drink again; he again found comfort in the bottom of a glass.

CHAPTER 3

Jimmy knew he had to pull himself together for the sake of Yvonne and little Steven , and after a few weeks he got offered a job as a steeplejack which entailed climbing up and repairing tall chimneys, which for a man with a drink problem was not a good career move, however it paid the bills. It was around that time that Jimmy started to show concern about Steven; he never used to go out and play with his friends and spent most of his time alone playing with his toys. He had no interest whatsoever in sports or exercise even when sometimes Jimmy used to ask him to kick the ball around the garden poor little Steven used to tire so quickly and always seemed to catch colds. He had no coordination with a bat or ball and no matter how hard he tried, Steven could not kick a ball to save his life.

With an increasing concern about his shortness of breath, Yvonne took him to the local medical centre to see his GP. He informed her that little Steven had asthma; he was also anaemic and always looked pale and thin. Steven started school 2 months after his 5th birthday, he attended Middleston primary school but his attendance was woeful as he was often absent due to catching whatever illnesses were going around. Poor little Steven struggled through primary school and then when he was 11 he started Middleston Comphrensive School which was made up from children from all over the town. Steven hated this school even more than hated his primary school he was now feeling even more vulnerable as he was one the youngest and weakest children in the whole school. He used to count the hours so he could go home to the safety of his mum and dad and used to run home as fast as he could which used to leave him totally worn out.

It was one such evening when he was running home that he would encounter someone who would make his life unbearable, his name was Dale Wilton, the school bully. He was in the 2nd form at Stevens school, Wilton was very tall for his age reasonably well built and had 2 older brothers who were also bullies, his brothers Greg and Billy were 16 and 17 respectively and had both been expelled from school and were both currently in a young offenders prison nearby. There reputation was fearsome and they would use violence to get there own way and were not to be messed with. Wilton was a nasty piece of work that like all bullies, was rude, aggressive, bad mannered, and used his size to intimidate people. He used to have a little gang who didn't particularly like him but were too afraid too leave , he used to like stealing money from smaller children and used to hang around the local shops looking for his prey.

One night Steven was told by his mum to bring back a carton of milk on his way home from school. Steven had went into the shop and bought the milk and proceeded to leave the store. As he walked out of the shop, minding his own business, Wilton was stood at the exit and stuck out his leg, tripping Steven over. He fell head first onto the floor as he dropped the milk carton, Wilton and his crew were amused and stood laughing at him. Steven got up and reached down to pick up the carton when Wilton kicked the carton clean out of Stevens hand with force, the carton spilt and the milk went everywhere. Steven ran home as fast as he could and when he arrived home he was exhausted and weak, he told his mum he had dropped the milk and the carton had split open , she told him not worry and poor Steven went to his bedroom and cried.

The following day Steven had a feeling Wilton would target him again , and he was right, Steven walked into the school gate still feeling the effects of the previous nights ordeal and straight into Wilton and his gang. they started to shout things at Steven, things like "don't cry over spilt milk wimp" and it was from that moment that Stevens life became hell. Steven couldn't wait to get back home to the safety of his home and his parents, but the days were going to get even longer now that he had became one of Wiltons targets. When school ended Steven rushed out as soon as he could to get past the shops where Wiltons gang hung out. He walked as quickly as his poor little legs would carry him but unfortunately he was pursued by Wilton and his gang and they stopped just before he could reach his road.

Steven was circled by the gang and was set on by them, they punched and kicked him as Wilton took a hold of Stevens tie, he pulled it so tight Steven was about to pass out. Wilton had ripped off all of the buttons from Stevens shirt but Steven froze with fear and couldn't do anything but try catch his breath, when out of nowhere came one of the girls from Stevens school her name was Tara Baker. Tara was a popular girl at school she was very pretty and bright and very level headed she told Wilton to let go of Steven and as Wilton fancied himself as a ladies man, he let go in a bid to impress Tara. He led his gang away from the scene laughing and joking about what had just happened.

Tara walked Steven back to his house and reassured Steven that Wilton would get tired of Steven soon and pick on someone else. Steven arrived home and rushed straight upstairs to hide his torn clothing and wash the blood from his face, he came down stairs and his mum knew there was a problem but Steven just told her he had been play fighting with a friend. She knew he was not telling the truth but she let it go because she could see the pain etched in his face.

CHAPTER 4

Tara was wrong about Wilton leaving Steven alone. Wilton didn't like the fact that Tara had stuck up for him so he was determined to make Stevens life even more unbearable. Each and every day Wilton and his gang deliberately went out of there way to pick on Steven, they once ripped up his homework, stole his school bag and on one occasion they threw Steven into the garden of Mrs Golightly, an elderly lady in her 70s who was chair person of the local neighbourhood watch. She had witnessed Wilton and his friends doing this and come out of her house to give the bullies a piece of her mind. She helped poor Steven up, brushed him down and walked him home to his house. Steven and Mrs Golightly became friends after the incident and he used to wave at her to and from school. He even ran errands for her if the weather was bad. Despite being as frail and fragile as Mrs Golightly, Steven helped her and anyone he could.

Wilton didn't like being told off by Mrs Golightly, so the bullying still continued. It went on for months and months, they never left him alone. It became even worse when Tara again stepped in to stop them picking on Steven. One day things got even worse when Steven put his name down for the football trials for the school football teams, of which Wilton was team captain. On the day of the trials Steven turned up only to be criticised by Wilton and his cronies. There were two teams picked by the sports teachers Mr Lester and his assistant Mr Charles, the game started with Dale Wilton and Steven on the same side and from the kick off Wilton did nothing but shout and abuse poor Steven who even though he tried his best he was hopeless and after 20 minutes, Steven was worn out and and to go off. He got changed and went home dejected and sad.

When he arrived back home his dads car was on the drive so Steven sneaked into the house and proceeded to sneak to his room, he could hear raised voices so out of curiosity he listened at the living room door. His dad who had been drinking was telling his mum how he had just lost his job because his boss had caught him drinking in his lunch break, but it was the next statement that really hurt him. He overheard his dad make the following statements "what do we do now no job , and what about my son where did I go wrong he is so weak ,he cant do sports ,he is a disgrace". Stevens mum stuck up for Steven and it ended with Jimmy storming from the house on route to the pub. Steven had heard every word and he felt he had let everyone down there was only one person he felt he could talk to and that was Tara.

He made his way to her house, she was his last hope, he felt as if he had let everyone down and felt worthless. As he neared Tara's house he saw a sight that made him feel physically sick, he could see Tara in the distance she was stood very close face to face with another boy and that boy was Dale Wilton, Steven hurried away walking as fast as he could, he walked for miles he just needed somewhere quieter to be alone with his thoughts. He remembered Ghostie wood and carried on walking to the special place his dad used to take him when he was younger, the clearing where nothing grew, and the location that was so peaceful. He sat on the old tree stump where he used to sit with his dad all those years ago. For what seemed like hours he just remained sitting there, deep in thought. It was beginning to get dark but he wasn't scared at all and the stories about the place being haunted did not bother him at all, he knew he would have to go back home soon but he felt so calm there he was so relaxed he closed his eyes and drifted to sleep.

He was awoken by a whirring sound and then a soft droning noise. He looked into the sky just above the clearing and there was a brilliant white light and in the centre of the bright light was an oval shaped craft which seemed to be getting closer and closer by the second. Steven was rooted to the tree stump but still he felt no fear whatsoever as the craft seemed to come closer, hovering approximately 2 metres from the ground. Suddenly 2 white shapes alighted, they had deep blue eyes but no other facial features at all and they were both staring intently at Steven. Still Steven felt no fear at all, in fact he felt relaxed in there presence and he somehow knew he was in no danger at all from the white shapes.

One of the shapes spoke to Steven in a strange language he had not heard before but he could understand everything it was saying, the shape asked him why he was so sad and Steven told them the reasons, he told them all about the bullies and his dads problems and then to make things even worse Tara was with the bully Wilton. The 2 white shapes looked at each other and one of them said "we have been observing your culture for many years and we could never understand why your people spend there lives hurting one another time and time again and we have come to the conclusion that we may be able to help you, we will look into your problems right now". At that moment Steven felt he was being lifted from the floor and seemed to be hovering just off the ground, he then felt what can only be described as a tingling sensation go through his body and whilst he hovered one of the shapes said "what we have given you is precious and special but you must never use your gift to hurt anyone unless they hurt you first, it must be controlled and if possible also used to help other people, you will be monitored and you will not abuse what we have given you".

At that moment Steven returned from his sleep, startled, he jumped to his feet looking around into the trees. The white shapes and there strange craft had disappeared, he stood there for a few seconds in disbelief. Was it a dream? Did it actually happen? He wasn't sure, but he knew he had to get home as soon as possible otherwise his mum would be worried. He decided to run home, setting off as fast as he could, but for Steven being so weak, that would be a struggle. He started off at a gentle jog but after a few strides he increased the pace and much to his surprise he found he started to sprint. He even started to hurdle the fallen trees and branches with ease and much to his astonishment, he was soon home. He wasn't even out of breath! In fact just for good measure he hurdled his garden gate much to the surprise of his mum who was stood waiting for him on the doorstep to the house. Worryingly, she asked him where he had been, he told her he had been to Ghostie wood with some friends. With a doubtful thought in her mind, she never said a word, she was just glad he was home safe.

Steven was ravenous so his mum made him some supper which he ate like a hungry lion and asked for seconds, his mum had always struggled to make him eat and now here he wanted more. Steven went to bed this night knowing this the start of his new life, a life he could finally enjoy.

CHAPTER 5

The following day Steven burst out of bed had a hearty breakfast and set off for school, he had no fear at all of what may lay in front of him, in fact he was a new boy now. He could feel surges of energy rushing through his body and he loved the feeling immensely, yesterday he was a shy timid little boy, now he was full of life and confidence. The first person he seen on his way to school was Tara he smiled and said good morning she replied the same back but Steven still had the vision of her walking with Dale Wilton the previous night so he said goodbye and proceeded to run to school.

He was about to walk into the school gate when stood blocking his way was Wilton and his cronies doing there usual ritual of taking money from the smaller children, they spotted Steven and stood in his way , normally Steven used to shudder when he saw Wilton but now he had no fear of him at all so this time Steven side stepped the bullies with a body swerve that David Beckham would of been proud of and carried on to his class.

The day was going well, Steven even started to enjoy his school work! He studied hard and over the next few weeks his school work improved, and his appetite had improved so much he could feel himself getting bigger and stronger every day plus he could run for ever. He now had boundless energy and seldom walked any where he used to run at every available opportunity. His parents could see the change in him and were both overjoyed. He managed to stay away from the bullies as best he could and one day he noticed the football team were playing a pre season friendly at the school so he decided to watch, he stood and noticed Mr Lester, the senior PE teacher who was with his assistant Mr Charles who remembered watching Stevens dad Jimmy when he played in the premiership. Mr Charles enquired to the well being of his dad , and then added can you play football Steven , Steven shook his head and said no but he would like the opportunity to try, so Mr Charles told him to put a shirt on as it was only a friendly and they were already getting hammered 5 - 0 so it wouldn't make a difference to the outcome of the match.

Mr Lester shook his head in disgust because he remembered the trials a few weeks earlier and how useless Steven was, but Mr Charles persuaded him to give Steven another chance. With 15 minutes left to play Steven went on as sub, he replaced one of Wiltons gang, Lee Jones who was not best pleased to say the least. Also Wilton who was team captain, mainly due to Mr Lester's' fear of Wilton and his family, was shouting his disgust toward the sideline. Wilton barked out to his team-mates "don't pass to him he is clueless" so Steven spent most of the time waiting for a pass. Finally having enough of not getting a touch of the ball, he decided to get it himself , he tackled one of his own team-mates, much to everyone's amazement! He flicked the ball over an opposition defender put his head down and set off at full pace towards the goal and chipped the ball perfectly over the goalkeepers head into the back of the net. Everyone stopped in there tracks and couldn't believe what they had witnessed.

The game ended a few seconds later and Stevens goal was the talk of the changing room much to the delight of Mr Charles. Every one seemed to be happy all except for Wilton and his cronies , and back in the changing room Wilton grabbed Steven by the arm and pushed him into a corner, "your goal was a fluke , and you shouldn't of even been on pitch and you got Jonesy taken off" , Steven knew he was in trouble but still had no fear at all of these people and what they could do to him. He held his ground as they closed in , there was a shout from the back of the room, "stop right now" a voice bellowed, it was Mr Charles, "you lot back off" he said. Wilton and his gang stopped in their tracks, they knew they would be in serious trouble if they carried on. The school didn't tolerate fighting and bullying and they feared if they did carry on, they would be expelled and excluded from all the sports. Steven grabbed his clothes and went home , but he knew this was not going to be over.

CHAPTER 6

The following day Steven arrived at school early to avoid the bullies and went to speak to Mr Charles to thank him for giving him a chance at yesterdays game. Mr Charles said "don't mention it son you made my day when you scored that goal and by the way the season starts in 2 weeks so get ready to be part of the team", Steven couldn't believe his ears, he went to his class with a big smile on his face. Whilst walking along the school corridor, he noticed Tara and tried his best to avoid her as he was still upset that she had been out with Wilton. Tara called to Steven because she needed to talk to him, Steven stopped and listened to what she had to say and Steven was totally shocked, she told him that she had heard that Wilton and his cronies were going to beat him up badly and she managed to prevent this by agreeing to go out with Wilton on a date, but she soon found out that Wilton told lies about everything so she left him after 10 dreadful minutes in his company. She also added coyly that she really wanted Steven to ask her out but he never did. Steven couldn't believe it, one of the nicest girls in the school wanted a date with him!! He mumbled an excuse and went to class still on cloud nine.

the following week the team had a training session planned, Mr Charles informed Steven before hand to bring his kit, and the following day the full squad turned up to play the final practice match before the season opened with Middleston Comphrensive v Middleston Grammar, who had never been beaten by Stevens school in 10 years. In fact the last time the school won against the grammar team, Stevens dad Jimmy scored the winning goal.

The practice game comprised of two teams of eleven picked by the team captain and vice captain, which were Dale Wilton and Matt Pullis. Respectively Wilton had already told Matt Pullis not to pick Steven until last for fear of retribution, so Steven was the last man chosen by Matt. Steven wondered what Wiltons plan would be, he didn't have to wonder for long. Wilton decided to man mark Steven personally and proceeded to push and jostle Steven at every available opportunity, then just before half time Steven got a breakaway and set off down the right leaving the full back standing, he then rounded the goalkeeper and was just about to tap the ball into the empty net when Wilton jumped in with a two footed tackle from behind that caught Steven about knee high. Steven went down in a heap and the teachers ran to his assistance fearing the worst, Steven lay quite still for a few seconds and then jumped to his feet to carry on playing, he felt no pain whatsoever. Mr Charles sent Wilton off the field for dangerous play, Wilton was furious and proceeded to walk the sideline glaring at Steven like a wild animal, the game restarted with a penalty to Stevens team and the usual penalty taker Glenn Carroll passed the ball to Steven "here you take it you earned it" he said. Steven placed the ball on the spot and then proceeded to blast an unstoppable shot into the roof of the net.

Steven then took control and scored two more goals, one volley from the edge of the box and then a well placed header that left first team goalkeeper Nigel Lonsdale rooted to the spot, the game ended 5 - 0 to Stevens's team and every one talking about Stevens's hat trick, all except Wilton who still insisted he was lucky. Wilton knew he was being watched by Mr Charles so he kept his distance and he even refused to shake Stevens hand when offered it by Steven he just brushed past him mumbling obscenities. Steven got changed and went home as fast as he could. Steven walked in to his house and blurted out the words proudly "Dad I scored 3, I scored 3 goals" his dad shook his head looked at Yvonne and said "yes son in your dreams". Steven felt disappointed that his own Dad wasn't believing him "Dad seriously I did, I scored 3 goals" his Dad was becoming increasingly angered and shouted at him "that's enough, you can't play sport so stop lying to me Steven!" Steven tried again to get a word in but his Dad interrupted and said "please son no more lies". Stevens mum could see the hurt on his face and told him that it really didn't matter and that they loved him anyway, even if he couldn't play any sport. Steven was stunned, he never said another word to his parents and went up to his room and cried.

CHAPTER 7

Steven soon fell asleep but woke up at 6 am so full of energy that he put his trainers on and went for a run before breakfast, he ran at full speed and nearly knocked the milkman over. He ran for over an hour, none stop, and could have gone further but his mum always had his breakfast on the table for 7.30am and he was ravenous. Steven ate his breakfast and then ran all the way to school, when he reached the school gates he seen Tara and her pals and they all wanted to congratulate him on the previous nights performance. Steven got very embarrassed; he was not used to compliments being given to him, especially from the girls!

He started to make his way to his class and was walking along the corridor when he was man handled into the boy's toilets by Wilton and his cronies. He was pushed into a cubicle and expected the worst when Wilton punched him smack bang in his nose, Stevens nose started to pour with blood but surprisingly Steven was not scared in the least nor did he feel any pain. Wilton attempted to punch him once again but Steven had had enough and lashed out at Wilton and caught him square on his chin, Wilton fell back landing on the toilet seat. Steven then saw his chance to escape and he wriggled through the gang and hurried into his classroom. He put his handkerchief to his bloody nose to quell the bleeding and carried on as if nothing had happened, but it wasn't long before the story of the incident was all around the school and Steven knew that Wilton would not let it go away. the incident also got back to Mr Charles who pulled Steven to one side in the corridor and gave him some sound advice "watch your back son Wilton is like all bullies he will get you when you least expect it, so be aware and also if you need my help just ask, Wilton and his family don't scare me one bit, oh and by the way you had a great game yesterday keep it up son".

At lunch, Wilton's table was adjacent to Stevens and Wilton spent the whole of lunch staring at him with his evil eyes. Steven watched as Wilton stole other pupils' food and his table manners were appalling, he gulped down his food down like a hungry dog and then continues to steal food from other plates. He spent the next 10 minutes burping and belching, much to the amusement of his gang. This day Wilton had other things on his mind than showing off and making his friends laugh, he was watching Steven like a hawk and when Steven was walking back to his table with his tray, Wilton stuck out his leg and tripped Steven over. His lunch landed on the floor in a heap, ruined, Steven was angry but still he kept his cool he just picked up his tray cleaned up the mess and walked out of the dining room with the sound of Wilton's moronic laughter bellowing behind him.

Wilton was confronted by Tara who told him to grow up and leave Steven alone, Wilton swore at Tara and told her to mind her own business. She felt so sorry for Steven she ran after him to console him, but Steven just carried on walking and ignoring her. After school he headed for home, a gentle jog turned into a sprint as he dashed into his house and up the stairs into his room. Lying on his bed he asked God over and over again "why me".

CHAPTER 8

Steven didn't sleep much that night as he knew he may have to go through yet another ordeal the following day, so as usual Steven had breakfast with his mum put his school shoes in his sports bag, put on his trainers and ran to school. Sure enough the usual suspects were waiting outside school gates and right at the front was bully boy Wilton, Steven knew he would have to face this problem head on there was no where to hide. Wilton stuck his ugly face into Stevens and said "me and you tonight Howe back field 4pm be there if you dare", Steven looked straight back at him and said "I will be there". Steven knew from that moment he couldn't run away anymore.

It didn't take long for news of the fight to spread all around the school and as the clock turned 3.45pm Stevens's heart was racing with adrenaline, but strangely enough he still had no fear of Wilton. He knew he had suffered enough at the bully Wilton's hands and he knew this was inevitable. He would have to face his biggest fear head on so he made his way to the back field were he could see a large crowd already gathering. He could see Wilton doing his sit ups and press ups, basically showing off to the crowd, he was also backed up by his cronies about 6 or 7 in all. Suddenly Steven felt as alone as he made the long walk to the back field by himself when he heard a voice he knew;

it was Bernard Fuller, another one of Wilton's victims. Poor Bernie had gone through the same ordeal as Steven. He ran up besides Steven and told him he would stand with him. Steven told Bernie not to get involved, after all it was his fight and Bernie had been through enough already. Bernie was adamant he was staying no matter what the consequences were, Steven was flattered but he knew Bernie was no match for Wilton and his gang.

Steven made his way into the man circle were he stood face to face with Wilton, who by that time was shouting what he was going to do to Steven, and once he was finished with him, it was Bernie's turn. They walked up to each other and Steven put out his hand to shake Wilton's, Wilton pushed it away still shouting the odds and took a swing at Steven which Steven managed to evade easily. He remembered the words the white shapes had told him 'not to hurt anyone unless he himself got hurt first' so Wilton kept throwing punches but some how Steven managed to avoid them. Wilton was getting more and more frustrated and couldn't land even one punch on Steven until one of Wilton cronies ran into the circle and planted a kick right on Stevens calf. Steven fell to the floor in pain and Wilton seized the opportunity to dive on top of Steven and launch a tirade of punches into Steven faces. He knew then that he had to retaliate to prevent serious injury; he somehow found the strength to push Wilton so hard that Wilton found himself lying flat on his back with Steven now on top and about to hit back. Steven pulled his fists back to hit Wilton when he heard a voice he knew and respected it was Mr Charles, he had seen the crowd gathering whilst driving home and fortunately for Wilton he came back to stop the fight. Steven immediately stopped and got up to brush himself down. Mr Charles told every one else to disperse and go home and then warned Steven and Wilton that if this happened again they would be in front of the headmaster and disciplined accordingly. He then told Wilton to go one way and told Steven to go the opposite direction.

When Steven started walking home he bumped into a few of the onlookers and was surprised by some of there comments regarding the fight, one boy said "you have made our day today Howe we were all hoping you would beat the bully and we still think you could of done, and to be honest nearly all of the school were rooting for you everyone is getting sick of bully Wilton's antics". The following day Steven ran to school as usual but was stopped in his tracks by Tara Baker, she said she wanted to speak to him so he stood still and listened to what she had to say , she told him "Steven I thought you were so different from the rest but you have come down in my estimation", she had heard about the fight ,and continued, "you brawling with Wilton, why didn't you just go home" Steven agreed but also emphasised that he had no choice he couldn't keep backing down , Tara walked away in disgust leaving Steven sad and confused. The next person he seen was Wilton stood in his usual spot outside of the school gate were he could steal money and food from vulnerable children, Steven was aware Tara was watching so walked up to Wilton held out his hand and apologised. Wilton give the same response as the previous night, he pushed away Stevens hand and proceeded to verbally abuse him with a tirade of obscene language.

Steven carried on walking and Wilton shouted after him "it's not over Howe I never forget ". The next person Steven saw was Mr Charles who seemed to be monitoring the situation from a distance, "Morning

Steven" said Mr Charles "I was hoping I would see you today, I have chosen the team for the first game of the new season and you are playing", Steven was on a high, he couldn't believe it and couldn't wait to get home and tell his mum and dad. After school had finished he ran home to tell his parents the good news but when he got there his mum was not there but his aunt was. Steven asked were his mum was and with a solemn look on her face she replied "Steven she is at the hospital. Your Dad has had an accident at work he had fallen from some scaffolding whilst erecting a platform, he is serious but stable and we are waiting for news from the hospital, so there's nothing we can do except wait and hope". Shocked and finding it hard to accept the news, Steven went to his room and got down on his knees and prayed for his Dad to be okay. Steven attended church every week, so surely God would protect his dad for him

For the next few days the family could only wait and hope, Steven decided to stay away from school, what would be the point he couldn't concentrate on his school work anyway. Two days after the accident, Stevens mum arrived home from the hospital with some good news and some bad. His dad had opened his eyes for the first time and he was now out of danger but he may never walk and could be in a wheelchair for the rest of his life. Steven was just pleased that his dad had survived and breathed a sigh of relief. The next day he went back to school as usual with his mind at rest and he was ready to concentrate on his school work again.

CHAPTER 9

That coming Saturday was the day of the big game against the Grammar School and the whole school was talking about it. Steven was more concerned about his Dad than any football game and went to tell Mr Charles that he couldn't play. Mr Charles told Steven to consider his decision as he had two days left before the big game was to be played. That night Steven and his family went to see his Dad in the hospital and whilst there, Stevens Mum mentioned the game to Jimmy, Stevens Dad. He smiled and said "you must play son it's just a shame I cant be there to see you" then he added "you can wear my boots, the pair I wore when I made my England debut". Steven was ecstatic and, the next day he told Mr Charles of his decision to play. Mr Charles was pleased and informed him that he would be in the starting 11, so the following day Steven spent hours cleaning and polishing his dad's old boots. He tried them on and they fit like a glove. The day of the big game was here and Steven was extremely excited.

The game was to be played at Middleston FC's training ground which was called The Spire; it was named after a local landmark which was an old oak tree shaped like a church steeple. The Spire had 8 full size soccer pitches including all weather pitches, Astroturf and a state of the art gym running track, and an indoor area where the first team would train. The team were told to be at the ground for 1.30pm for a 3pm kick off. Steven arrived at 1pm, put his kit away and went on a run around the track. He needed to clear his head everything was coming too fast and he found a good run usually did the trick. He finished his run when the rest of the lads turned up and they all went the changing room where Mr Charles and Mr Lester were to give there team talk. With team talks over Mr Charles named the starting 11 but when Stevens name was read out Wilton gave out a big sigh and shook his head in disapproval. He then stood and said "as Captain of this team I would just like to say you are making a big mistake in selecting Howe, you have selected him on one lucky game and one fluke of a goal. If he plays we will get beat he is useless!" After his rant, Wilton sat down still shaking his head in disgust, Mr Charles intervened and said "the team is picked and it will remain the same nothing more to be said about the matter" and then added "right lads lets go outside on to the pitch to soak up the atmosphere".

There were around 2 hundred spectators present including Stevens Mum and her parents, Stevens's grandparents Jack and Mary. Just on the half way line, Steven spotted Tara Baker, she waved and he waved back to her. She giggled with her friends as Steven felt butterflies in his tummy just thinking about her being there. The boys returned to the changing room to get ready for the big game, but when Steven looked in his bag his boots had gone, his Dads boots. Mr Charles noticed the look of horror on Stevens face and asked what the problem was, Steven told him his boots were gone, Mr Charles asked the rest of the team to check there bags, but it was no use his boots had been stolen. Steven was devastated, he pleaded with who ever took them to return them but no one owned up. Wilton spoke up and said out loud "what's the problem they were ancient anyway you should have got yourself a new pair" Steven then knew who had stolen his boots because no one had seen them, they were tucked away inside of his bag so how could Wilton know they were old? Mr Charles also noticed that when the lads went for a walk onto the pitch Wilton was not present, but that would have to wait, they had a game to play. "Right" said Mr Lester "you can wear these boots they may be too big but its all we have" passing Steven some boots. Steven put them on but couldn't hide his sadness for losing his dads boots and the significance of them.

The game kicked off with Steven playing in his usual centre midfield position and he received the ball just outside the opposition's box. He had time and space to fire a shot at goal but completely missed the ball and fell flat on his backside much to the amusement of some of the crowd , Steven couldn't stop thinking about his Dads boots and how upset his Dad would be when he found out. Thirty five minutes into the game, Steven received a throw out by his Goalkeeper, Nigel Lonsdale, but he was dispossessed by a Grammar school striker who scored with a low drive, 1-0 to the Grammar School. Steven couldn't wait for the whistle to blow for half time; he knew he was having bad game. At half time Wilton stated again that Steven was rubbish and should be taken off and substituted immediately, but Mr Charles told him to keep quiet. Mr Charles knew that Steven was upset about his boots so decided to give him another chance he said quietly to Steven, "I am going to give you 15 minutes to prove yourself I want you to do it for the team but most of all do it for your Dad". Steven knew he had to pull himself together and play well, so he started the second half in a more positive frame of mind.

Steven tackled and chased every player and opportunity of possession of the ball, and on 50 minutes, won the ball on the half way line. He jinked his way past 3 defenders and then chipped the ball over the keeper from 25 metres to equalise and make the score 1-1. The Grammar School then turned up the heat and attacked but found Goalkeeper Nigel Lonsdale in great form, and then on 88 minutes Steven went on another mazy run only to be brought down in the box. He was awarded a penalty but Dale Wilton grabbed the ball and placed it on the spot, he wanted to score the winner himself. He blasted straight down the middle but the keeper managed to push the ball out, but out of nowhere Steven followed up to score the rebound and that proved to be the winner, 2-1 to Stevens's team!

They managed to hold on to record the win, the first one in 10 years. Mr Charles and Mr Lester were delighted and everyone was on a high all except for Dale Wilton who strode away from the celebrations with 5 members of his gang in tow. Steven noticed this and couldn't help but think what other stroke Wilton would have up his sleeve and he knew he couldn't let down his guard. That night Steven and his Mum went to visit his Dad at the hospital and Steven told him about his 2 goals. His dad was so happy and replied "I hoped my old boots helped". Steven didn't have the heart to tell him about the boots being stolen so he just smiled and said "yes dad they did". That night, with his dad getting much stronger, Steven went out for his usual pre supper run and managed to knock 30 seconds off his previous best time. He was getting faster and stronger each and every day and after he showered and ate his supper he settled down to watch TV with his mum.

There was a knock on the door the door, Stevens mum went to answer it and in the doorway stood Tara

Baker. She had come to congratulate Steven on his performance that afternoon. Stevens mum invited her inside, the three of them chatted for about an hour until Yvonne got tired and went to bed leaving Steven and Tara alone to talk. Tara told Steven of her feelings toward him and Steven couldn't believe someone as pretty as Tara could be interested in him. What he didn't realise was that he had developed into a good looking young lad; he also had developed his body shape and had a lovely physique. From that day forward, Tara and Steven became inseparable.

The following day Steven ran to school as usual but when he reached the school gates he was greeted by Tara she looked pale and in distress. "Steven have you heard about Bernie Fuller he was beaten up last night, he is in hospital. He was attacked by a gang of lads on his way home and is in a bad way". Steven knew when Bernie stood with him when he had trouble with Wilton a few days earlier that it may have repercussions but didn't expect it to be so bad. The next person he seen was Wilton, he was laughing out loud and telling people how him and his gang had beaten up poor Bernie Fuller. He glared at Steven and said "your next Howe, and by the way my dogs enjoyed eating your boots". Steven couldn't help himself he strode towards Wilton and his gang he didn't care about the consequences all he could think of was poor Bernie lying in a hospital bed and he blamed himself. Wilton and his cronies started to circle Steven, but Steven had no fear at all of them. Just as they were about to clash Tara ran between them and shouted to Steven to stop and immediately Steven stopped turned around and walked to his class shaking with rage. Wilton started to call after Steven "your a chicken Howe you hide behind your girlfriend" Steven knew he couldn't take anymore things would have to come to a head.

That night Steven and Tara went to visit Bernie in hospital he was covered in bandages and had a plaster cast on his left arm. He told them the gory details of the attack and how he had tried to run away but had fallen over and how he could hear Walton's voice orchestrating the attack which ended with the gang holding his left arm outstretched whilst Wilton jumped up and down on it until it broke. Steven was furious but Bernie told him to calm down and not allow things to escalate. Bernie had suffered enough and Steven knew this so he said he would let things go. Whilst he was at the hospital he also paid a visit to his dad, his mum was already there and he was greeted by the good news that his dad would be coming home the following week and that cheered him up no end.

CHAPTER 10

The following week was the start of the schools football season and the football squad was training hard. Mr Lester and Mr Charles were very optimistic about the oncoming matches and really thought they had a realistic chance of finishing quite high in the league. So they stepped up the training regime to 3 nights per week. Steven revelled in it, he loved to train, the more he trained the better he felt and the stronger and fitter he became. He had developed a friendship with the team goalkeeper Nigel Lonsdale who as well being a goalie was also a promising amateur boxer. He was also a boy Wilton stayed away from after all even bullies know there limits.

Nigel never looked for trouble; he was more concerned with his schoolwork and his family. One night after training Nigel told Steven he was going on to the boxing club for a quick session on the punch bags and the and told Steven he could go with him. Steven wasn't sure as he was a bit wary of strangers and new surroundings but Nigel told him that he would be made welcome by all and the coaches were the best in the business. Steven agreed and rang his mum to tell her he would be late home and off they went to Middleston Amateur Boxing Academy. Nigel was well respected there by students and coaches alike. He introduced Steven to everyone and whilst Steven looked on, Nigel started his routine of 3 minutes non stop punching on the bags and pads.

Nigel was very good he was fast and accurate and hit with power and precision he done 3x3 minute rounds and then stopped for a water break and get some well earned rest. One of the coaches, Jon Worton, said to Steven "go on son you have a go", Steven wasn't sure but Nigel egged him on "go on Steven give it a try". Steven donned the gloves and off he went he started very slowly, it was all about hand to eye coordination, so at first he missed the pads completely and felt like giving up. He started to relax a little and he soon got the hang of it, Steven started to catch the pads with speed power and accuracy and that brought the attention of the rest of the boys plus the other 2 coaches Mally Dryden and Jim Cosgrove.

Stevens's punches were getting even faster and he was hitting even harder, in fact every one stopped what they were doing and stood in amazement at this newcomer, he was a natural. He carried on for a full 10 minutes and could have carried on longer but Jon Wortons hands were to beginning to hurt from holding the pads so he called a halt to proceedings. Steven turned around to face the rest of the boys slightly embarrassed by his actions and the rest of the boys started to clap, they were shaking there heads in utter amazement. Jon called a halt to the session and everyone got showered and dressed and then sat around whilst Jon, Mally and Ritchie gave them a run down of there session. The first question asked by the coaches were to Steven and they wanted to know how many bouts Steven had fought, Steven felt rather embarrassed then he replied none at all. Astounded, Jon went on to say how well Steven had done and asked him if he would be interested in joining the academy.

Steven said he would have to ask his mum and dad first before he could give them an answer.

Steven ran home as fast as he could and told his mum the good news but his mum told him he would have to ask his dad because she did not like violence in any shape or form. Steven wouldn't have long to ask his dad, as he was coming home the very next day.

CHAPTER 11

The next day Steven sprinted to school as usual, he was on a high knowing his dad was coming home and as usual the bullies were in there positions stood just outside the school gates ready to pounce on there prey. Steven couldn't be bothered to run the gauntlet so he took a run up and vaulted the iron fence with ease and landing with the poise of gymnast on the grass of the school field. The bullies couldn't believe there eyes at what Steven had just done. Steven calmly composed himself and walked into his class, he had avoided them yet again. When he was going for his lunch he bumped into Nigel Lonsdale and Nigel was buzzing about his boxing abilities and asked when he would be coming back to train there, Steven said he would have to get his dads permission first. Steven walked home from school and couldn't wait to see his dad back home were he belonged.

When he arrived home his dad was sat in his favourite chair he ran to his dad and hugged him it was as if he had never been away, they ate dinner together just like before and Steven thought the time was right to ask his dad about the boxing academy. He asked his dads views on the matter and the answer he got surprised him, his dad replied "yes son I have no problem with that at all in fact my father used to box at a good standard and took me to the same academy when I was a youngster but I was more into football than boxing so I left to concentrate more on my football, but I have no problem with you going boxing in fact I encourage it". Steven looked at his mum and she just shook her head and sighed out loud she didn't approve of violence in any shape or form but she trusted her husbands judgement completely so it was agreed that Steven could begin his boxing training as soon as he wanted to.

The schools football season started the very next day and Steven couldn't wait to get started. The first game was away to Blakesworth School, a team that were always difficult to beat at there own ground. They also had a midfield player called Michael Murphy playing for them and Michael was being scouted at that time by several league clubs including his home town team Middleston FC. Their chief scout Harry Jameson was attending the game to watch Michael with a view to him being offered a full time contract with the club so there was quite a crowd assembled to watch.

Mr Lester and Mr Charles had selected the team to start and Steven was playing centre midfield with Damien Taylor and Matt Hollis either side of him and Amir Haider playing on the left wing. Dale Wilton was Captain as usual due to the influence he had over Mr Lester. Blakesworth kicked off and the ball soon found Murphy on the edge of the box, he tried to chip the ball over Nigel Lonsdale but Nigel showed his agility and saved it well. He then proceeded to launch the ball up to his two strikers, Peter Nottley and Neil Donavon but the ball was cleared by a Blakesworth defender. At half time the game was 0 – 0, then on 50 minutes a bad clearance by Wilton was seized upon by Murphy who put the ball into the back of the net beyond the dive of Lonsdale, 1-0 to Blakesworth. The game was pretty much even when Murphy took on three defenders and had only the keeper to beat when from out of nowhere, Steven nicked the ball from him and set off on a run that can only be described as amazing.

He set off at pace leaving 3 defenders in his wake somehow flicked the ball over the centre back and without even changing pace drove the ball past the Blakesworth keeper to make the score 1-1. He then started to organise his team mates around him he knew they could win this game, and on 80 minutes he sent Peter Nottley away with an inch perfect pass that only had the keeper to beat and Nottley blasted the ball home 2-1 to Middleston with 2 minutes left on the clock. Steven again took control and knowing that they had to keep possession to win the game, held on to the ball near the opposition corner flag despite being tackled ferociously by the Blakesworth players. His plan succeeded when the ref blew his whistle for full time, 3 points to Middleston.

The Middleston team were ecstatic, they had beaten one of the league favourites on there own ground, a truly memorable feat, all except dale Wilton who shouted to Steven "I am the Captain of this team Howe, I will give out the instructions not you". The rest of the lads carried on with there celebrations. Mr Charles and Mr Lester were also very pleased with the result but Mr Charles told the lads to calm down, he knew it was a hard season ahead and would now know that they were the team to beat. He told the lads to focus on the next game which was at home midweek against St Josephs RC School who always had a strong team but with no injuries to report he was quietly confident.

CHAPTER 12

The following Wednesday night the football squad met at the sports hall with Mr Lester and Mr Charles to discuss tactics and name the team. As expected it was the same team apart from Mr Charles named Steven Vice Captain after his performance against Blakesworth. Dale Wilton objected vehemently and shouted his objections against the decision stating that Steven was just a one game wonder, but previous Vice Captain, Matty Hollis had no objections at all, and he accepted the decision knowing that it was for the good of the team and in the long run may prove to be the right move. St Josephs were good strong team and in midfield they had the fastest player in the league his name was Lee Armstrong. He ran for the county and could run the 100 metres in less than 10 seconds so the game was evenly balanced and just before kick off Mr Charles spotted Harry Jameson the chief scout for Middleston FC and wondered which player he had come to see. It wouldn't be long before he was to find out.

The game kicked off and the ball was pushed back to Steven from Neil Donavon. Steven sidestepped two lunging tackles to play a glorious pass right to the feet of Amir Haider who took on the opposition full back to get in a cross. From out of nowhere Steven arrived to head the ball like a bullet, it passed the keeper to open the scoring 1-0 to Middleston. St Josephs tried to get back into the game when a ball from their centre back set Lee Armstrong away. He had a 10 metre start on Steven but somehow Steven not only caught up to him he also took the ball from him as he was about to shoot for goal.

Steven then turned, put his head down and set off at full pace from his own box to the opposition box taking on 5 defenders on his way and unleashed a shot into the back of the net from fully 30 metres. The keeper could only stand and watch as it went in the net, 2-0 to Middleston. It was then Harry Jameson made his move, he walked up to Mr Lester and Mr Charles and said "who the hell is that kid, I watched him play last week but only seen a glimpse of him" and at that moment Steven executed a perfect over head kick, 3 - 0 to Middleston.

After that, Steven ran and chased every ball and delivered a slide rule pass to Donavon to make it 4-0, then with the full time whistle about to be blown, Steven volleyed home a cross from Amir Haider to make it 5-0. Game over. Harry Jameson asked for permission to talk to Steven and of course his teachers agreed to it. Mr Lester asked Steven to wait around a while until the other boys had left and when they had gone, Harry Jameson walked in and said "you played well, so well in fact I will attend your next game with Middleston FC's Assistant Youth Team coach Rob Bolton, I have just rang him and he will accompany me to the game to specifically watch you play. I have told him of your potential and he is very interested". Steven was gob smacked; he couldn't believe this was happening to him.

Steven ran home to tell his parents the news, they

were both excited about this and Steven rang Tara to tell her. The next day it was all around the school and most of the school were happy for Steven all except for Wilton who never hid the fact of his hatred and jealousy of Steven. God knows what evil plan he was thinking up at that time but Steven was clever enough to know this and he knew he would have to be on guard at all times.

That night Steven met Nigel Lonsdale for boxing practise at the academy. Steven loved the boxing training and whilst he was there, boxing coach Mally Dryden wanted to see Steven spar with some of the more experienced boys. He told Steven to put in his gum shield and spar, he put him in the ring with schoolboy champion Sam Healy who had a record of 19 bouts which included 17 wins and 2 draws and no defeats. Mally instructed Sam to go easy on Steven so off they went and Steven knew he couldn't hit anyone first, he just done his best to avoid being hit.

Steven had an unbelievable awareness of where his opponent was going to attack and simply dodged everything that Sam could throw at him until the second round when Sam caught him with a slightly dubious low punch which allowed Steven to make his move. He delivered a three punch combination that stopped Sam in his tracks. Sam had been hit so hard and fast that he never even seen the punches coming. Mally had seen enough, he pulled Sam out and sent in another 2 of his best boxers and the same thing happened to them. The first fighter, Steven stopped with a body punch and the second with a sharp right hook to the head that dropped his opponent on one knee.

Steven had just achieved an unbelievable feat and when he turned to face the rest of the academy who were by now watching the sparring session, all he could see were the rest of the boys shaking there heads in disbelief. There was a strange quietness in the academy until Jon worton started off a tumultuous applause and every one started to clap. An embarrassed Steven from the ring Mal and Jon knew they had unearthed a real find in Steven and Mal asked Steven if he would box on the next boxing show that was being held in 3 weeks time at the town hall. Steven said he would have to ask his parents permission but couldn't see any problems with that.

Once he was home he had a shower, ate his dinner and then asked his parents about the boxing show. His mum wasn't sure but his dad was more than pleased to agree to his request. Steven phoned Mally Dryden and told him the good news, now it was up to Mal to find a suitable opponent for Steven. Steven had other things on his mind and that was the following week-ends football match for his school team, coupled with the knowledge that the game was going to be attended by not only Harry Jameson but also Middleston's Youth Team coach Rob Bolton and he knew that a lot rested on him having a good performance.

CHAPTER 12

Stevens's team were to play a team from another city in the county cup in their next match. That team was Kenton College. They were last season's county cup winners and a good hardworking team full of very good individual players that combined well as a team so it would be Stevens's toughest test to date but he was up for it. Now it seemed nothing fazed Steven he was just getting stronger, fitter and faster every day. He ran everywhere and even when watching TV with Tara he do sits ups and push ups.

Stevens's team were playing at home to Kenton and nearly all of the school would be there so before the match Mr Lester and Mr Charles tried to keep the boys as calm as possible and then named the team. It was the same team that won there last with one exception, Mr Charles told the boys Steven would Captain the team, Wilton started to shout rant and rave at the top of his voice. Mr Charles told him to keep quiet or he wouldn't be playing at all, "in fact" Mr Charles added "in the last game you were terrible you didn't encourage the team and your overall performance was very average" Wilton stared over at Steven and said under his breath "this is your fault, I will see you later, your going down".

The lads changed into there kit and Steven proudly

put on the Captains armband. They had their team talk and the Referee told them to make there way onto the pitch. They stood in file with Steven at the front, Mr Charles and Mr Lester had gone out to make a space and keep the crowds at bay when Steven felt a terrible pain to his left calf muscle he turned around and Wilton was being pulled away by Nigel Lonsdale and Vice Captain, Matty Hollis. He had waited for his opportunity to attack Steven and seen his chance and took it; he had kicked Steven from behind on his calf. Steven turned around to confront Wilton but Nigel shouted to Steven "we have a game to play leave it Steven please". When the ref came in and repeated his request "onto the pitch lads", Steven knew it would have to wait and somehow hobbled his way onto the pitch to the cheering crowd.

Mr Charles noticed Steven limping and asked him if he was okay, Steven replied "yes I am okay sir, no problem" but Steven could feel his calf muscle getting tighter by the second. Strangely he couldn't feel any pain.

Steven won the toss and kicked off attacking the school end and could see from the corner of his eye Harry Jameson pointing at him with another man who must have been Rob Norton. The ball was played back to Steven who attempted to control the ball when his calf muscle went into spasm and he mistimed his control and the ball went out of play for a throw in. Rob Norton looked at Harry Jameson and shook his head "you may have got this one wrong Harry" he said, poor Harry couldn't understand what had occurred but he told Rob to be patient. Steven then received a deliberately miss timed pass from Wilton and faced with an opposing player and due to his injury, he lost the ball completely and Kenton scored a goal.

Steven stayed down after the challenge and had to be carried off the field for treatment from Mr Charles who was also a qualified physio, "your calf is badly bruised Steven what's happened back there in the changing room", "nothing sir nothing at all" Steven replied , "you cant go back on you will make it even worse Steven" said Mr Charles, "just put some ice on it sir I have to get back out there were getting beat", hesitantly, Mr Charles agree to let him back onto the field, telling him he will give him until half time and if his leg was no better he will substitute him. Steven looked up to the sky and asked for help, he knew how important this game was for him and his family. He closed his eyes and wished out loud "please help me", he felt a surge of electricity go through his body and he knew the white shapes were listening and watching him. He jumped up and said to Mr Charles "I am ok sir just get me back on the field" Mr Charles couldn't believe what he had seen. Steven was jumping up and down and pumping himself up to get back on the pitch, the Referee beckoned him back onto the pitch just when his team defending a corner kick.

Middleston had been under real pressure since Steven had gone off and his team mates were certainly glad to see him back. The corner kick flew into the penalty area and was going straight toward the Kenton centre forwards head when Steven leaped up even higher to clear the ball to safety. The teams turned around at half time with Kenton still 1 - 0 in the lead plus they had nearly all of the possession and should have scored more. They turned around with Kenton to kick off the second half, Kenton had decided to try and keep possession and had put nearly everyone in defence to try and go for a 1 - 0 win. It looked like their plan may have worked until the 81st minute when Steven sent Donavon clear and he was fouled just outside the box.

Free kick to Middleston. Wilton lined up to take his usual speculative blast at goal when Steven nipped in before him to slot the ball precisely in to the corner off the net, 1-1.

Instead of being overjoyed at his team getting the equaliser, Wilton grabbed Steven by the throat, Steven by that time had just about enough and threw Wilton with ease straight to the floor with a perfect judo throw. The Referee gave Steven and Wilton Yellow cards and warned them to calm down. Wilton was so surprised how easily Steven dealt with him he walked away like all bullies do when you fight back. The game carried on at a lightening fast pace and on 85 minutes, Steven latched on to a pass from Richard Kent to chip the keeper 2 - 1 to Middleston. Again on 89 minutes, Steven took on six defenders but refused to give up the ball and cheekily rounded the Kenton keeper to make it 3 - 1 to Middleston. After the game Mr Lester took Steven and Wilton to one side and warned them that there behaviour would not be tolerated within the school rules and asked them to shake hands. Steven put out his hand but Wilton pushed his hand away and walked away from him. Mr Lester was still wary of Wilton and his family so said nothing.

CHAPTER 13

The whole school was on a high as were the staff, Tara was so proud of Steven's achievements as were his mum and dad, and to cap a memorable day Harry Jameson called to Stevens home to ask his parents if they would mind if Steven could sign forms to play for Middleston FC's Junior team. They were delighted of course and agreed immediately so Stevens's life was beginning to get better. However life throws up more problems when you least expect them and bullies like Wilton only go away when you stand up to them and show them you are not afraid of them.

The following week Wiltons' brothers were due out of the youth prison and they were a nasty piece of work. Steven knew he would have to be extra careful when they were released back into the community. Dale Wilton's brothers were Greg, aged 17 and Billy, aged 18. They had both been in the young offenders institution for violence and had been grooming there younger brother Dale to follow in there footsteps. They also had a gang who terrorised the locals from the area; the gang was called the South Side Crew named after the area they came from, South Side Estate. Everyone knew they were coming out and knew what to expect from them, they were all hoping that their spell being locked up may have changed them.

The following Friday, Greg and Billy stood outside of the school gates to greet their brother Dale, there were about 10 of them in all and were laughing and joking with each other. When Steven walked out of school you could have cut the tension with a knife, Dale had been writing to his brothers and they knew all about Steven. Steven was just about to walk past the gang when Mr Charles who had anticipated problems walked out of the gates, "Steven" he called, "we need to discuss tactics for tomorrows game, can you come in and discuss them with me now". Steven had a lucky escape. The Wilton's walked off toward the town centre looking for some one else to terrorise instead. Mr Charles let Steven go but told him to be careful and never let his guard down around the gang. Steven agreed with Mr Charles but strangely enough was not scared of the Wilton boys or anyone else for that matter.

As soon as he arrived home, he rang Tara. She had started college a few weeks earlier and was studying sport science. She ran with Steven most nights even though he had to slow down to enable her to keep up and he called her to see how her day had gone. Steven had his dinner and watched TV for a while then went to bed in anticipation of the game the following day. Stevens's team were playing away to Northwood School in a league game. Northwood had a notorious sloping pitch and it was very hard kicking up the hill but Northwood had mastered it to a fine art. If they won the toss they would always kick downhill first half score as many goals as possible and then weather the storm and defend their lead in the second half. It usually worked a treat; they had only lost one game in 5 seasons so Steven knew it was going to be difficult.

Stevens's team lost the toss and as usual Northwood kicked down hill but Mr Charles had a plan, he was going to play with 5 at the back instead of the usual back 4 and the fifth man at the back was going to be Steven alongside Wilton and maybe, just maybe, Wilton and Steven might be friends after this. Wilton showed his dismay toward this decision with his usual ranting but Mr Charles told him to get on with it or come off.

The game kicked off with the team getting bombarded by long high balls pumped into their goal area by Northwood, but Wilton and Steven coped admirably until Wilton decided to go on walkabout. He knew Steven would struggle with long high balls that were being hurled at him and despite the shouts from Mr Lester and Mr Charles to go back and defend, he never. After 10 minutes gone Northwood took the lead when due to Wilton's walkabout, it led to Steven having to leave his man and tried to cover for Wilton, it left their striker to score past Nigel Lonsdale 1 - 0 to Northwood then on 30 minutes, Wilton cleared the ball deliberately to a Northwood forward who scored again to make it 2-0. It was then that Steven made a decision, he decided to go for every ball and try and keep Wilton out of the picture, so he did just that. He won every header and through ball. At half time it was still 2-0 to Northwood who when they turned around played with a blanket defence of 10 men behind the ball at all times.

Mr Charles instructed Steven to play upfront and try and pinch a goal back but he was being man marked by three Northwood defenders, they had obviously heard stories about Steven and his goal scoring prowess. Steven was being pulled and pushed by all 3 of them in a bid to prevent him even receiving the ball, but 75 minutes on the clock a long through ball by Matty Hollis eluded the Northwood defence and Steven saw his chance and set off like a greyhound to outstrip there defence. He chipped the ball over the keepers head, 2-1 to Northwood. This seemed to rattle the Northwood team and Steven could sense a win. He turned with his back to goal and even though he was still marked by 3 defenders, he flicked the ball past them and unleashed a thunderbolt shot past the keeper to score 2-2 with 5minutes left to play.

Being urged on by Mr Lester and Mr Charles, Steven ran full speed at the Northwood defence and got inside the box when he was upended by a defender which resulted in a penalty to Middleston. Steven put the ball down to take the kick, took 3 strides back and waited a second. He then placed it with pace and power into the back of the net 3-2, which proved to be the winner. Middleston had achieved a great away win against a very strong Northwood team, everyone was happy apart from Wilton especially when he got a rollicking from Mr Charles for not defending well in first half and his momentary lapse of concentration which led to Northwood's goal. He never even looked at Steven or congratulated him.

CHAPTER 14

The following Wednesday was the night of the academy's boxing show and Steven was feeling a little nervous to say the least. He was matched against Jonny 'the tank' Lowther who was well up in the rankings in amateur boxing. Maybe Malcolm and Jon had pushed him too far ahead of himself. Jonny was known as 'the tank' because of his strength and power and had only lost once in the 10 bouts that he had fought, but the coaches had good reason to do this, they had seen enough of Stevens ability to know he was special and they had arranged for boxing promoter Toni Visconti to be present to see for himself Stevens ability.

Steven had butterflies in his tummy whilst he waited to be called into the ring and he could see his Dad and Tara in the crowd. It put him under even greater pressure knowing two people he loved were there to watch him. He had seen Jonny around the town from time to time and often thought he was a lad he wouldn't want to cross and now here he was going into the ring to fight him. But as usual Steven had no fear at all and when the bell went Jonny came straight at Steven looking for an early win but Steven went into defence mode and he couldn't land a single punch. A few minutes had gone by and finally Jonny hit Steven with a punch that rocked Steven down to his boots. Steven then knew he could now fight back and did; he caught

Jonny with a ferocious left hook which left him reeling but still on his feet.

Steven knew he could finish it there and then but he couldn't hurt anyone just for the sake of it so he held back and let Jonny regain his composure. Everyone in the crowd knew he could have ended the fight and couldn't believe that he had not. Again Jonny came on the attack and caught Steven with a right cross that shook him again so Steven knew then he would have to finish the contest to avoid being hurt, so he hit him back with a 3 punch combination that saw Jonny go down on one knee, he was winded badly and couldn't carry on. The Ref awarded the fight to Steven on a TKO, Technical Knock Out. Steven had 5 more fights that month and won every one convincingly. Toni Visconti attended every one of his bouts then out the blue Steven got a call from an excited Mally Dryden, he told Steven he had been selected to fight for Great Britain against the USA team that was touring Europe at the Wembley arena.

Steven jumped at the chance to represent Great Britain, the fight was to be held in 2 weeks time and Stevens's parents were very happy, even though his mum wasn't sure as she loathed violence in any shape or form.

Steven still captained his school to 3 more football victories, one cup game and two leagues which put Middleston Comp top of the table. On the day of the boxing international Steven was feeling on top of the world, Steven left home at 6am for the long drive to London; he had to go to the weigh in first before his big fight. He was accompanied by Mal and Jon and Nigel Lonsdale for support. Steven decided to take his pal Bernie Fuller with him too. Stevens dad followed at 10 am with Stevens mum and Tara. There was a huge crowd in attendance at the arena, and the USA team was full of very talented boxers including new golden gloves champion Warwick 'Lightning Strikes' Sykes, he was expected to turn professional straight after the tour with the top promoters queuing up for his signature. Tony Visconti had already offered him a contract too.

The contest started with USA taking a 2 -0 lead then Great Britain pulled it back level 2 - 2. Then G.B took a surprising 3 - 2 lead when Scotsman Will Hunter won on points. Following this, the USA team put in their more experienced and heavy weighted fighters and won 2 more rounds, making it 4 - 3 to the USA. With only 2 bouts left and still to use Lightning Sykes, they looked certain winners but again the Great Britain team pulled it back to 4 - 4 with one more bout to go. With Sykes still awaiting his chance, Steven was told to get ready as he was in the ring next. He knew this was the decider round and that put even more pressure on him. The USA team sent in Sykes to be Stevens's opponent.

Sykes was taller than Steven and had a reach advantage he was also heavier. He had also got a record of 30 straight wins no defeats with 28 knockouts under his belt but still Steven showed no signs of fear at all. If anything, he was more determined to savour the moment than worry about how much bigger and experienced Sykes was. He was determined to savour the moment come what may. The fighters stood face to face in the ring, the crowd by this time were at fever pitch and the noise was deafening. At the bell, Sykes as expected, went on the on the attack. His hand speed was unbelievable but he still had yet to land a decent punch on Steven and at the bell Sykes was ahead because he was on the attack more than Steven.

The second round was the same, Steven knew he could not land the first blow so he decided to wait for the counter punch and it came early in the third and final round. Sykes caught Steven square on the jaw with right cross; Steven shook his head and now knew he could show his stuff. He walked forward taking 5 more punches as if they never happened then fired off a 5 punch combination that knocked Sykes onto the seat of his pants. Sykes attempted to get up but was so stunned his legs wouldn't cooperate. Steven had won by a knock out and Great Britain had won the contest because of it. The crowd went crazy with applauses, whistles and shouting. Steven went back to his dressing room through a mass of well wishers to where his mum, dad and Tara were waiting for him. Toni Visconti also was there. He had in his hand a preliminary professional contract and pleaded with Stevens parents to allow Steven to sign.

CHAPTER 15

Stevens's dad had seen many contracts in his time and asked for a month or two to let Steven make up his mind. Visconti agreed to this because he knew he had witnessed a star in the making and did not want to lose him, but when Visconti had gone, Steven looked at the amount he was being offered just to sign. It was enough to pay off all of the family's debts and some left over. He told his dad this but his dad insisted he wait also Steven already had a contract albeit a temporary one with Middleston FC Junior Football Team so there was a lot of thinking to be done.

The weekend arrived and Steven had another football game to play for his school. The opposing team was called West Park Secondary and Mr Charles had already been told that there were Scouts from five different Premiership Football Club teams attending the match, including Middleston FC's Assistant Manager, Tommy Reece. Through the grapevine he had also heard that they were attending the match to watch Steven. Word soon got around that Tommy Reece was in the crowd and Steven knew this could be his chance. Tommy Reece was at the game on the insistence of chief scout Harry Jameson, who had seen qualities in Steven from an early age. Steven was determined to not let anyone down.

Middleston School won the game 9-3 and Steven scored 7 goals. Steven played awesome, his power and pace were electric and when he arrived home after the game there were 5 premiership scouts parked outside of his home. Stevens's dad gave everyone of them a chance to speak but deep down he knew Stevens mind was already made up and Tommy Reece, who knew Stevens dad from his time with Middleston several years ago, offered Steven a semi pro contract immediately. They shook hands and arranged for Steven and his dad to attend a meeting at their training ground, The Spire, with team manager Ian McDonough and Club Chairman Sir Roger Stoker.

Steven was taken on a tour of the training complex by Sir Roger and offered terms providing he passed the medical the following week. The next day it was in the local press with headlines of "local boy about to sign pro forms for city" and everyone was happy about this with the exception of one person, Dale Wilton, who was reading the headlines out to his brothers. "We must do something about this" Wilton said, his brothers agreed and started to devise a plan to ruin Stevens chances of becoming a professional footballer.

In the meantime Steven had started playing tennis with Tara at the local sports centre, he found tennis very different to football and boxing and at first struggled just to return Tara's serve, but as usual he soon got the hang of it and after a few more weeks he started to enjoy it. One night, there were another couple on the next court, Tara and Steven got talking to them and the other couple suggested a game of doubles. Steven and Tara had been watching them as they played and they looked very good but Steven loved a challenge so they accepted. The couple joined them on their court and proceeded to play taking a 3 games to love lead, but again Steven soon got the hang of things and he started to hit the ball with pace, accuracy and power. Steven and Tara managed to win the first set 6-4 and then Stevens fitness shone through and they won the next two sets 6 – 2.

After the game Steven and Tara had a coffee with the other couple and they asked Steven how long he had been playing tennis for. Steven replied telling them that it was only his third time ever playing the game. The other couple shook there heads in disbelief and insisted that he must have had lessons, explaining that he hit the ball with such precision and served well. Steven replied "I never have had lessons before, honestly". The couple couldn't believe that he was such a natural at a sport like tennis. They shook Stevens hand and said "you could go a long way, why don't you join a tennis club, you could get even better " and with a smile on his face the guy said to him "but I still think you have had lessons", they all laughed and went there separate ways.

Steven took Tara home and proceeded back to his house. He was about 500 metres away from his home when he saw Wilton stood with 2 of his gang so he crossed the road to avoid him. All of a sudden he was grabbed from behind by Wilton's brothers he was pushed into a wall, he gained his composure and turned around, only to be confronted by Dale Wilton, his two brothers and two members of the gang. They were armed with baseball bats and one of them had a knife in his hand, Steven knew he would have to fight for his life, there was no way out, he was surrounded and out numbered 5 to 1.

Wiltons brother Greg threw the first punch which caught Steven full in his face he knew then he could, and had to fight back. He went into fight mode and used all his boxing skills to the full effect and even though he was being punched, kicked and struck by baseball bats, he couldn't feel any pain whatsoever. After what seemed like forever, but was only about 30 seconds, it was all over. Wilton's two brothers and there two accomplices were lying in a heap on the floor but where was Dale Wilton?? Steven was soon to find out he had ran off fearing the worst and had stopped a passing police car telling them he was being attacked.

The police arrived and all they could see were four youths lying in a heap covered in blood and Steven was stood over them. Steven was arrested and taken to the nearby Police Station and held there on suspicion of assault. He was kept in a cell overnight and released on bail the following day. Whilst in custody, Steven was allowed a phone call to his parents and they were waiting for him when he got out to take him home. His mum was fraught with worry but his dad knew he was innocent and they both embraced. They drove straight home as his dad asked him what had happened. Steven told him the truth that he was attacked by five youths and had to fight for his life. Steven went to his bedroom and sat in a daze, thinking about how much he hated being locked up in a cell and the noise of the other prisoners shouting all night. He hadn't slept a wink and soon fell fast asleep. He was awoken just after lunch by his mobile phone ringing, it was Tara, "Steven" she said "it's all over the local newspaper you have been arrested by the police are you all right" Steven said he was okay but still in a daze about what had actually happened the previous night. When the evening paper arrived he got an even bigger shock the headline was "young starlet arrested, four youths in hospital", he was stunned. Just when things were going great this happens, but this was only the start.

CHAPTER 16

Stevens dad received a phone call from Sir Roger Stoker and team manager Ian McDonough asking what the situation was, then Mr Charles called to the house to see if Steven was okay, Steven told Mr Charles the full story and Mr Charles believed him as he knew the Wiltons history. He knew their father was a well known local bully who was in and out of prison for assault charges. He said he would help anyway he could. Stevens's dad informed him about the calls from Sir Roger and Ian McDonough and told him that if these allegations were true they would have to review their offer of a contract and the medical would have to be put on hold for this was a serious allegation. Steven was dis-heartened; everything he had been working hard for could now be taken away from him. If he was proved to be guilty, he could go to prison too.

He was told to attend the police station the following week where he was formally charged with grievous bodily harm, Steven froze with fear, and the first time he had ever felt fear in a long time. He knew he could be in serious trouble and for the time being Steven felt like he had the weight of the world on his shoulders. When he arrived home he couldn't take it all in and he couldn't even think straight anymore, he had to get away from everyone for a while. He went to a place he loved and hoped would help him think straight and relax. He went to Ghostie wood. He ran as fast as he could to the clearance in the trees where he went all those years ago. As he sat on the old tree, he watched as the sky turned from an ocean blue to a midnight black, he closed his eyes and started to drift to sleep.

He was woken by familiar voices; it was the white shapes that had visited him years before. They told him they knew of his dilemma and they would help him get through this ordeal. Steven woke up startled, frantically looking around in hope of seeing the white shapes still there. Much to his surprise, the only person that was there was his dad. He was stood in front of him and softly said to him "I knew you would be here son, we were worried about you, lets go home your mum and Tara are concerned about you". Steven stood up looked up to the sky and quietly said thank you, his dad didn't say a word.

In the days that followed, Stevens's parents decided to stop Steven from attending school and the following week Steven had to attend the Magistrates Court where he was again bailed to appear at Crown Court two weeks later. Those two weeks were sheer hell for him, he never left his home and was under immense pressure but he had friends visit him, good people who believed in him totally. All of the football team turned up with the exception of Wilton, for obvious reasons. Most of the boxing academy lads including the coaching staff Mally and Jon. Mr Charles was a frequent visitor, along with Bernie, Nigel Lonsdale and of course Tara. She stood by him and his parents throughout the whole ordeal. One day Steven had a much unexpected guest, Jonny 'the tank' Lowther turned up to see him! Jonny had the utmost respect for Steven and knew that when he fought Steven 6 months previous, that Steven could have hurt him badly, but only just done enough to win. Jonny hated bullied and he knew that Steven would never intentionally hurt someone.

Stevens's dad had been in contact with a Solicitor regarding Stevens's court case and the case went ahead as planned. The Wiltons were still carrying there bumps and bruises but were all fit enough to attend Court. Maybe with the knowledge that if they won the case, they were all going to get substantial amounts of money from the Criminal Injuries board. The Wiltons stood in the witness stand and told lie after lie, they said they were walking home when they were set upon by Steven. They explained that they had backed down but he trapped them and beat them up. They also blamed Steven for the possession of a knife and baseball bat which explained the extent of their injuries. However there were no knifes or baseball bats found at the scene so it was Stevens word against theirs.

Steven looked like he could go to jail, he sat with his head in his hands as he thought to himself that his whole world was about to come crashing down on top of him. The case seemed to be getting worse and worse until someone called out from the public gallery, it was Mrs Golightly, at first the Judge ordered her to be quiet and Stevens Solicitor went to speak to her. He come back with a DVD disc in his hand and explained to the Judge that he thought he should see this. The judge, the prosecution, the defence barrister and the chairman of the Jury went into the Judges chambers whilst the court usher set up the DVD player. He pressed play as the DVD started. Everyone in the court room gasped, shocked by what they saw, Mrs Golightly had seen Wilton and his gang hanging around outside her house and suspecting they were up to no good, recorded the whole incident entirely.

The DVD showed Steven crossing the road to the opposite side to where Wilton and his gang were stood; he was trying to avoid any trouble, not cause it. The DVD played on and showed the gang attack Steven using weapons. It showed Steven having to defend himself to stop being badly hurt but only hitting back when he had to, it even showed Wilton creeping back later to pick up the weapons and take them away to destroy evidence. The judge was angry and went back into court and acquitted Steven of all charges. The case was dismissed and there were no charges to answer. He then apologised to Steven for the anguish he had been through and summoned the Wiltons to be tried for perjury and wasting taxpayers' money. They were all bailed for 6 weeks for social reports and Steven walked out of the court room a free man and into the arms of Tara and his mum and dad.

CHAPTER 17

That night the newspaper had different headlines "Wonder boy walks free from court", and that night his phone never stopped with well wishers congratulating Steven. Over emotional and relieved that it was all over, Steven walked to Ghostie wood to his favourite spot, got down on his knees and thanked everyone for there help. He said a special thank you to the white shapes as they had told him everything would be okay and it was. The next day Steven was accompanied by his proud father to sign professional forms for Middleston FC, he passed his medical and he had finally made it. When Steven went back to school he had the same reaction from the rest of the pupils, they were all pleased he was free and that his life was back on track. The Wiltons were even more raging towards Steven and determined to wreck his life. Dale and his brothers realised they were going to prison so they planned one last scheme to mar Stevens future. Billy Wilton knew some unsavoury characters from his time in prison, one of them being a lad from the next town who was fearless. He offered him money to take Steven on and he agreed, but they knew Steven wouldn't fight; he had too much to lose. That afternoon, with Dale Wilton being expelled from school, he and his brothers, along with a gang of around 20 youths, waited for Steven outside of the school gate. Steven walked alone out of the school and couldn't believe his eyes "not again" he sighed "please not again". The gang circled Steven and this time he knew he couldn't win.

The gang came toward Steven waving there fists, ready to fight. Steven was blocked in by the gang, he couldn't get out and if he tried, he knew he was going to get hit by at least one, if not all of them. All of a sudden the gang stopped and looked past Steven, and when Steven looked behind he could not believe what he saw. The whole school were stood behind him, the full football team and even the boxing academy boys had turned up too. They had all received a text that apparently one of Wiltons gang had told someone that Steven was going to be cornered after school by over 20 lads. With everyone fearing for Stevens's safety, they rounded everyone up and ensured that Steven would be okay. Even 'the tank' had turned up to protect him.

Steven could see the fear in Dale Wiltons face and he knew then it was all over. Wilton turned around and like all bullies he ran away and the rest soon followed. Steven knew at that moment he was free from Wilton forever. That night Steven went to Ghostie Wood to thank the white shapes for all of their help, but when he closed his eyes there were no voices, no shapes, nothing. Maybe they had gone as they had 'done their job', or maybe they were never really there in the first place? Just a figment of a vulnerable little boy's imagination? You can decide for yourselves. But remember you and only you can make it happen and only you can decide your own destiny.

Steven went from strength to strength, he decided not pursue his boxing career as it meant hurting people but carried on with Football. He made his debut for Middleston FC aged just 16. He then went on to Captain them when he was just 18 years of age. Steven then became England's youngest ever captain at 19 years old. He represented his country at all levels and was capped by his country 88 times in all and scored an incredible 125 goals. Steven was named European Footballer of The Year 10 times and World Footballer of the Year on 8 occasions. On the day he made his full England debut he requested and was allowed extra seats for his parents, Tara, his closest friends, which included Nigel Lonsdale, Bernie Fuller, Jon Worton, Mally Dryden, Mr Charles, and of course Jonny 'the tank' Lowther. He and Tara got married on his 25th birthday and they had three children, 1 girl and 2 boys. His dad Jimmy had a successful knee operation and now can walk unaided and runs marathons in aid of local charities. His mum Yvonne now runs a successful charitable organisation that helps children who suffer from bullying at school. It is funded by England captain Steven Howe.

ABOUT THE AUTHOR

I am a kid from a council estate that strived for better things in life, i had a rough upbringing but somehow survived ,through willpower stuborness not to let the bullies win ., i found my inspiration from within myself and through my own self belief and my never say die attitude.

27875861R00044

Printed in Great Britain
by Amazon